ALLEN COUNTY PUBLIC LIBRARY

3 1833 0491 2242

P9-ECT-084

Me!

Philip Waechter

Handprint Books Brooklyn, New York

Me.

I like myself.

I enjoy life and I know my own mind.

I take things at my own pace.

I'm super.

I place great emphasis on personal appearance.

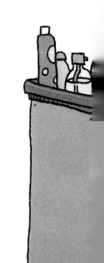

I'm beautiful.

I enjoy the little things in life...

. . .and, of course,
the big things too.

I speak many languages. . .

. . . and feel at home
everywhere in the world.

I love surprises. . .

. . . and I'm up for anything.

I'm terribly brave.

"GRRRR

Fearlessly, I face life's challenges.

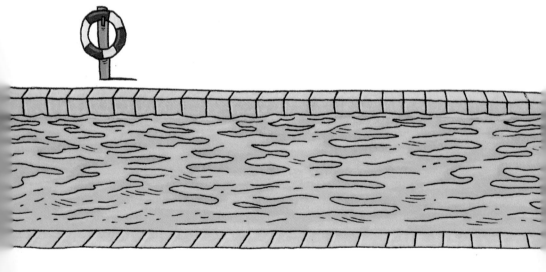

In fact, I'm afraid of no one and nothing.

Well, hardly nothing.

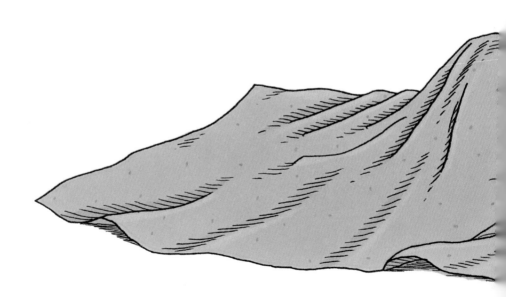

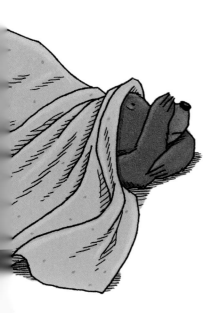

Generosity is my middle name. I love to share.

I have a big heart . . .

. . . and everyone loves me.

On top of everything, I'm clever.

I guess that makes me pretty special.

But still there are days . . .

. . .when I feel absolutely alone . . .

. . . and small.

That's when I head for the road . . .

. . . and run . . .

. . . and run . . .

. . . to you.

I'm glad you're here.

Copyright © 2004 by Beltz & Gelberg
Translation copyright © 2004 by Christopher Franceschelli
All rights reserved · CIP data available
Published in the United States 2005 by Handprint Books
413 Sixth Avenue, Brooklyn, New York 11215
www.handprintbooks.com
First U.S. Edition
Originally published in Germany by Beltz & Gelberg
Printed in China

ISBN 1-59354-087-6

2   4   6   8 10 9   7   5   3   1